# The Happy Crab

Layla and Kevin Palmer

Illustrated by Guy Wolek

BETHANYHOUSE

*a division of Baker Publishing Group*

Minneapolis, Minnesota

**To Steevenson—you sparkle like sun on the sea!**



Published by Bethany House Publishers
11400 Hampshire Avenue South
Bloomington, Minnesota 55438
www.bethanyhouse.com

Bethany House Publishers is a division of
Baker Publishing Group, Grand Rapids, Michigan

Printed in China



Library of Congress Cataloging-in-Publication Data
Names: Palmer, Layla, author. | Palmer, Kevin Lee, author. | Wolek, Guy, illustrator.
Title: The happy crab / Layla Palmer and Kevin Palmer ; illustrated by Guy Wolek.
Description: Minneapolis, Minnesota : Bethany House Publishers, [2021] |
Identifiers: LCCN 2021011625 | ISBN 9780764238550 (cloth)
Subjects: CYAC: Altruism—Fiction. | Happiness—Fiction. | Crabs—Fiction. | Seashore—Fiction.
Classification: LCC PZ7.1.P35713 Hap 2021 | DDC [E]—dc23
LC record available at https://lccn.loc.gov/2021011625

Cover design by Jennifer Parker
Cover illustration by Guy Wolek

Authors are represented by Lisa Jackson of Alive Literary.

Illustrator is represented by Jean Blasco of Blasco Creative.

21 22 23 24 25 26 27 7 6 5 4 3 2

**ONCE UPON A TIME**, there was a curious little crab who lived in the sea.

He loved to go on adventures so he could see new places and experience new things.

One time, he hitched a ride all the way to Haiti on the back of a giant whale.

Another time, he sailed across the Gulf of Mexico and found buried treasure on Pensacola Beach.

One sunny morning, he rode the waves to the Santa Rosa Sound where the water was super shallow and bubbling with stingrays swimming all around.

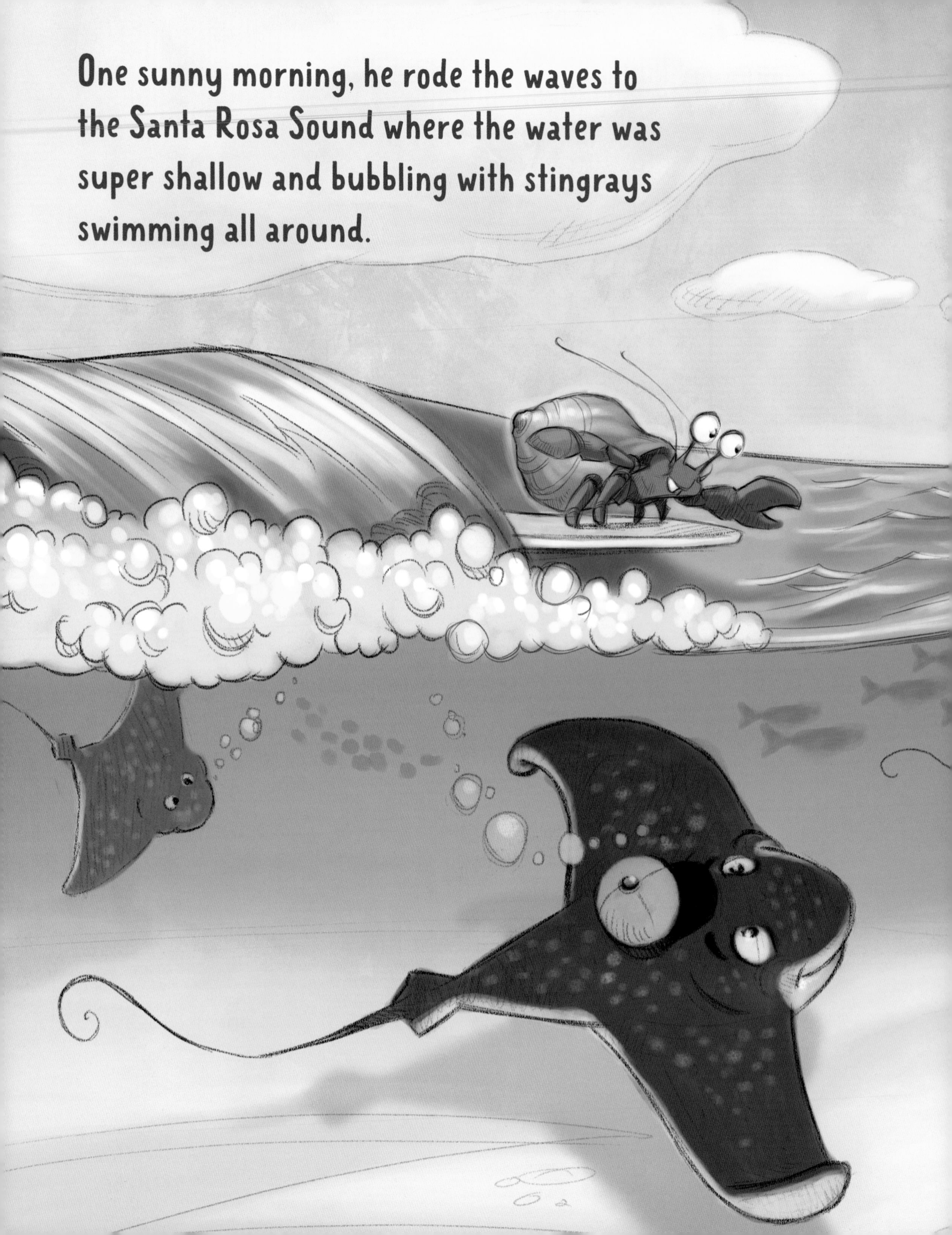

He saw fluffy old pelicans soaking up the sun and crafty little crabs building castles in the sand.

As he splashed in the salty surf and played with his new sea friends, he thought to himself, *Life is good!*

Later that day, the crab started to feel a little sleepy, so he tucked himself into his shell for a nap.

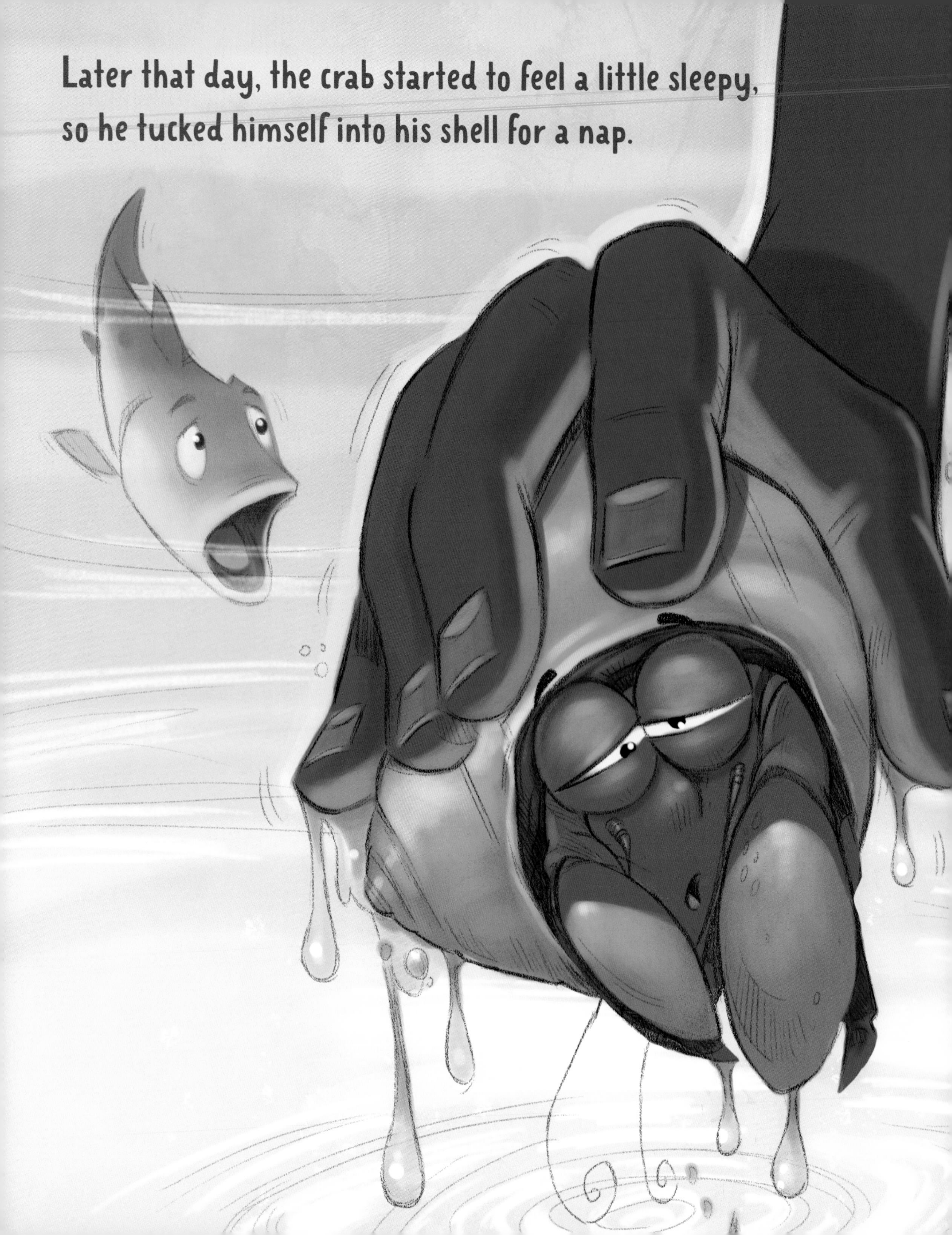

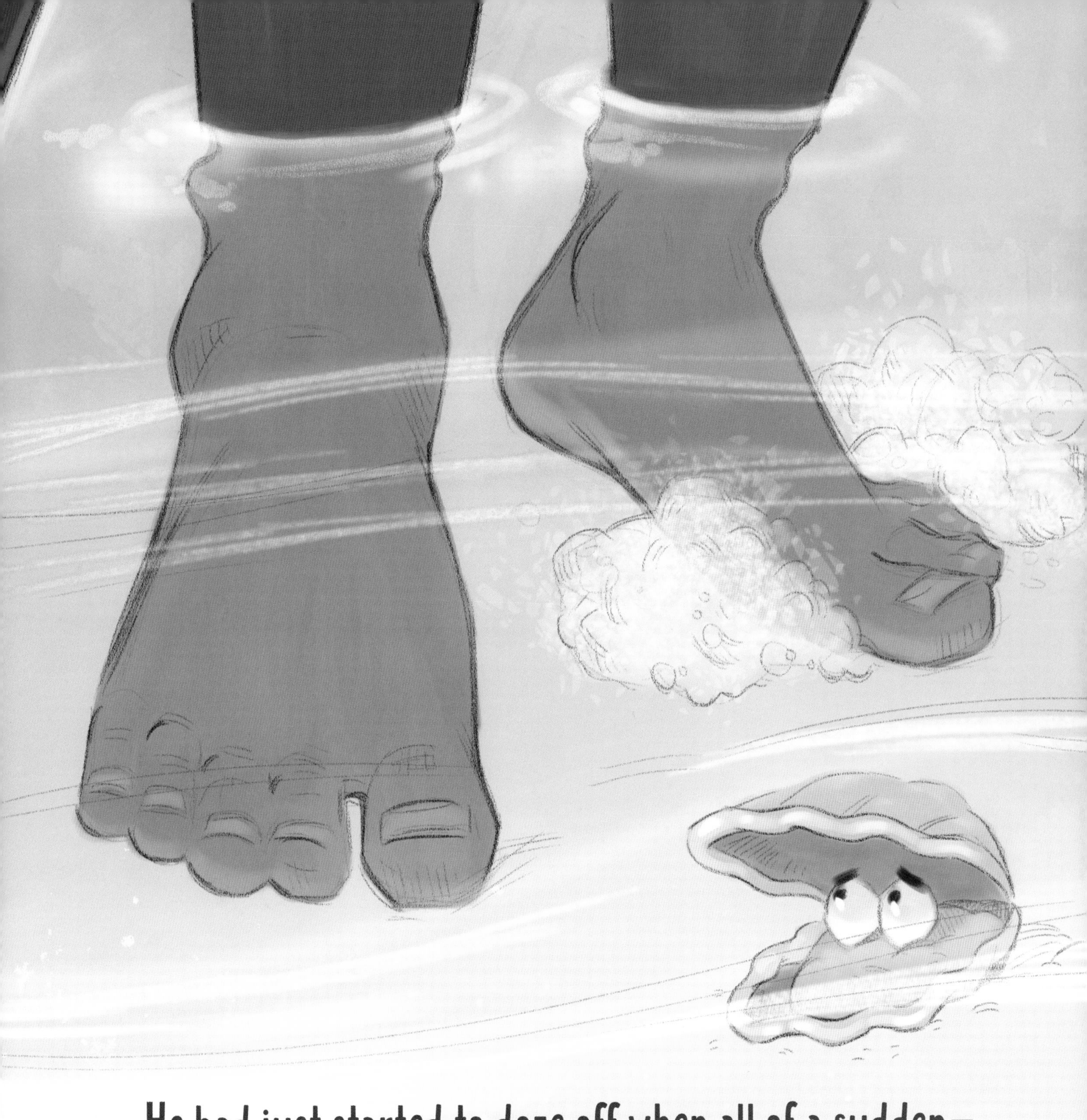

He had just started to doze off when all of a sudden—
WHOOSH! Up and out of the water he went.

*What's happening?!* he thought.

He peeked out of his shell and saw four people–feet standing in the water below. It was a mama and her son who had been walking along the shore and spotted his beautiful shell.

"It's so perfect!" he heard the boy say. "I can't believe it! We've never found a shell this big that wasn't broken. Can we keep it, Mama? Please, can we?"

"Sure, honey!" the boy's mama replied. "We'll keep it as a souvenir so that we can always remember this trip."

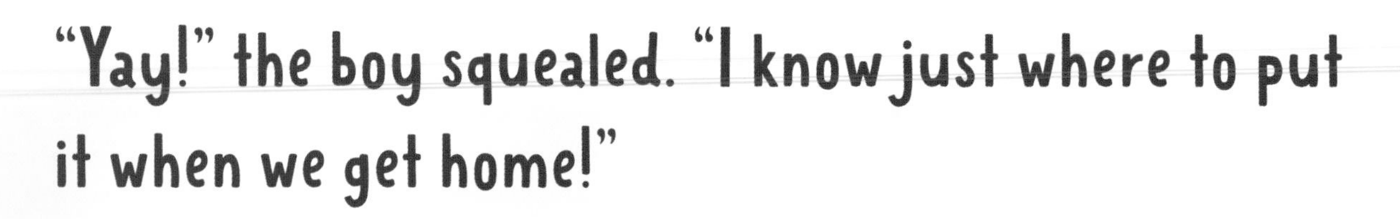

"Yay!" the boy squealed. "I know just where to put it when we get home!"

Hearing that, the little crab felt very scared and quickly hid deeper in his shell.

*Oh no!* he thought. *Where are they taking me?*

"It's time to go!" he suddenly heard someone call. "Okay!" the boy replied to his dad, who was packing up to leave.

"I'm going to hold it all the way home," the boy said to his mama.

*All the way home? What does he mean?* the crab thought. *The **SEA** is my home and I want to stay!*

As they drove away from the beach, the little crab became very sad and wondered, *Will I ever see my friends again?*

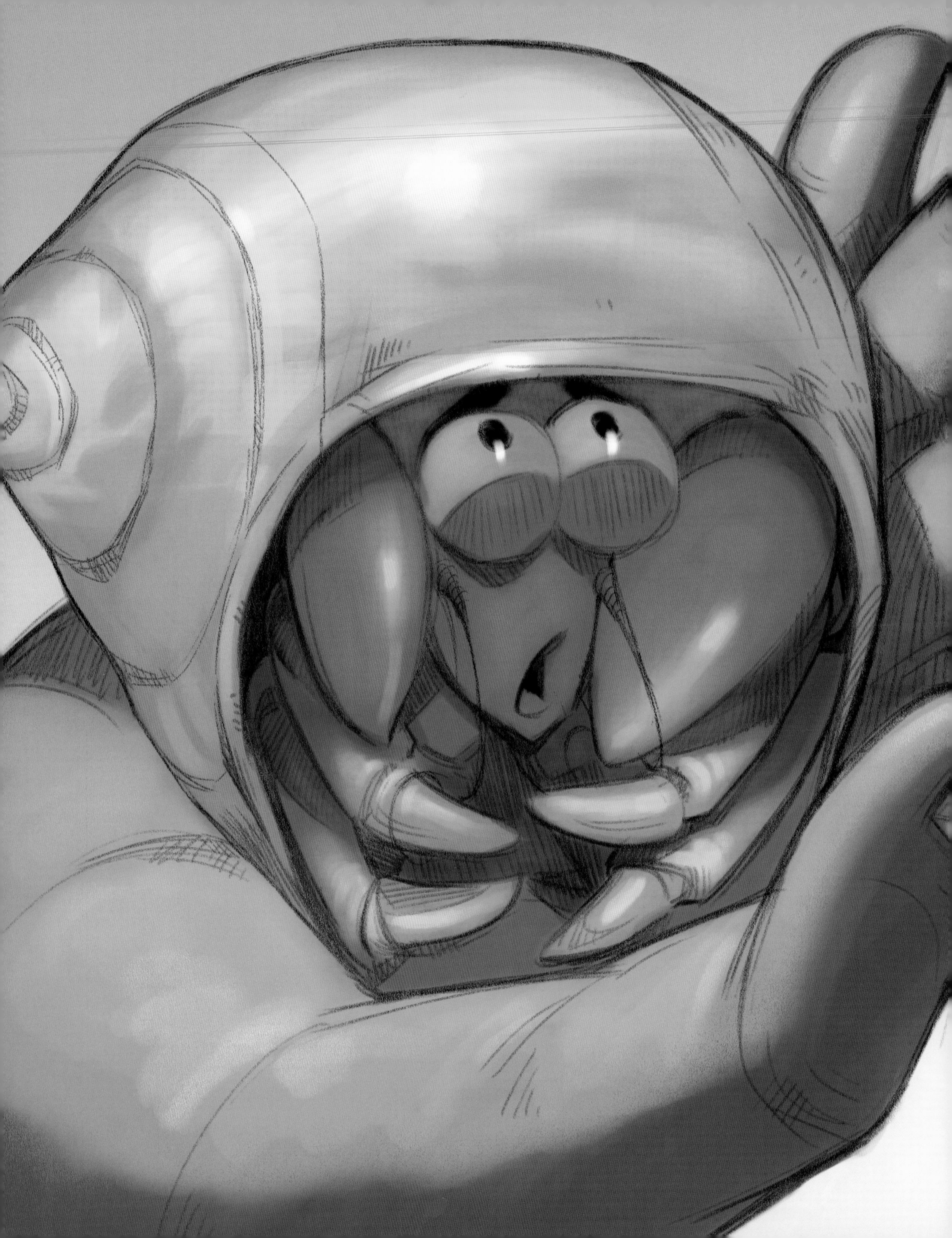

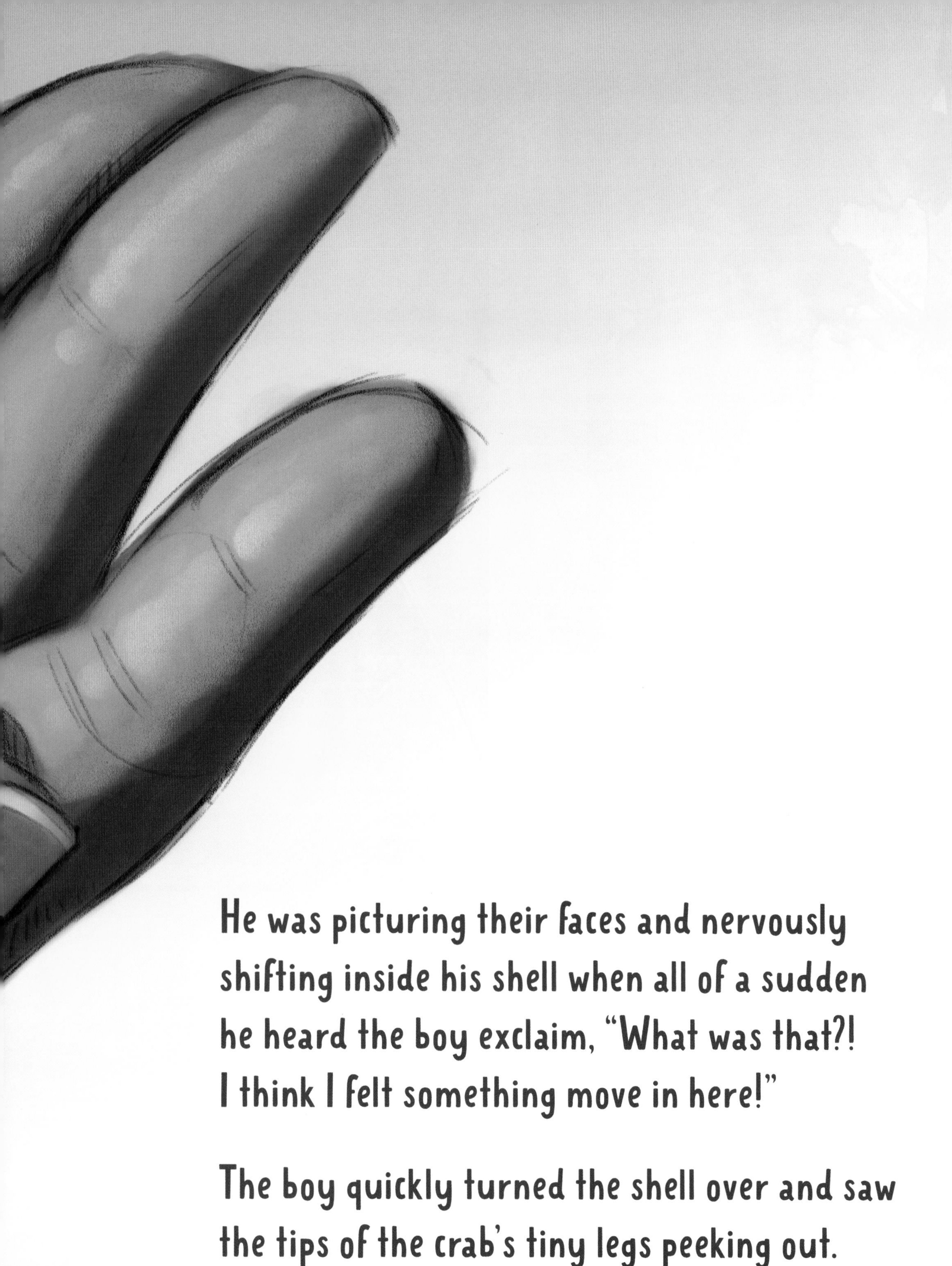

He was picturing their faces and nervously shifting inside his shell when all of a sudden he heard the boy exclaim, "What was that?! I think I felt something move in here!"

The boy quickly turned the shell over and saw the tips of the crab's tiny legs peeking out.

"Whoa," he gasped. "There's a CRAB inside this shell!"

"What?! Are you sure?" his mama asked as they continued to drive up the road.

"Yes!" said the boy. "I can see his toes!"

"Oh my!" his mama cried.

"Can we still keep it?" the boy asked.

"I don't know, honey," his mama replied. "This shell seems to be a part of him."

"But what if we never find a shell this perfect again?" the boy asked.

"Oh, sweetie, the ocean holds millions of perfect shells, and we can always look for more, but this shell belongs to the crab, and the crab belongs in the sea. Besides, *keeping* a perfect shell isn't what makes it so special. It's the thrill of *finding* one that makes an adventure so fun!"

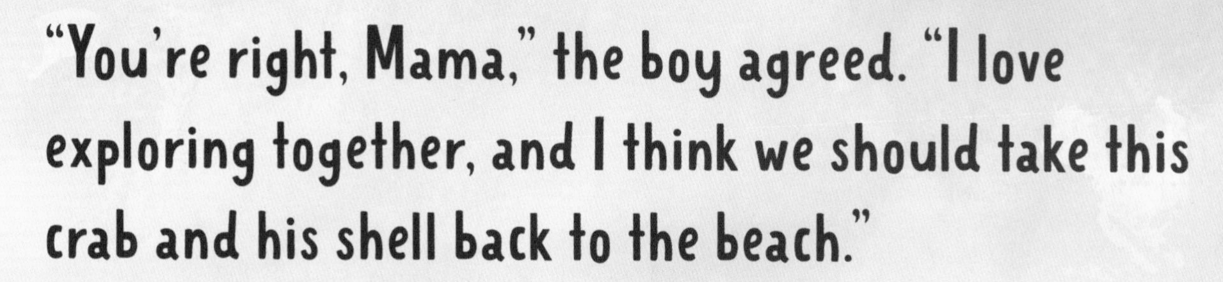

"You're right, Mama," the boy agreed. "I love exploring together, and I think we should take this crab and his shell back to the beach."

Hearing that, the crab breathed a big sigh of relief. Grateful for the boy's compassion, he smiled and thought, *This may be my wildest adventure yet!*

As the family rushed the crab back to the water's edge, he heard the boy ask, "Do you think I can name him before we say goodbye?"

"I think that's a great idea!" his mama replied. "What do you think his name should be?"

"Hmmm. I want him to be Happy," said the boy.

"You want him to *be* happy or you want to *name* him Happy?" asked his mama.

"BOTH!" exclaimed the boy.

"Happy it is!" said the smiley mama.

The little crab heard the good news and loved his new name, and when the next wave washed onto the shore, he knew it was time to go.

As the current carried him out to his next adventure,
a friendly stingray passed by and yelled,
"Hey! How are you?"

The little crab thought about his new friends,
and with a huge smile replied,

I'M

HAPPYYYY!